USBORNE HOTSHOTS

SOCCER SKILLS

USBORNE HOTSHOTS

SOCCER SKILLS

Edited by Alastair Smith and Paula Woods
Designed by Nigel Reece

Illustrated by Paddy Mounter
and Chris Lyon

Photographs by David Cannon (Allsport UK)

Consultants: David Shannon, Ian St John
and Frank McLintock

Series editor: Judy Tatchell
Series designer: Ruth Russell

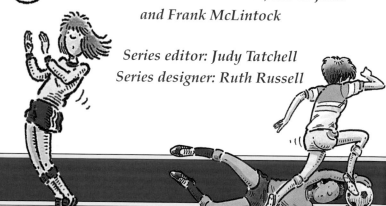

CONTENTS

4 Basic skills

6 Killing the ball

8 Passing

10 Shooting for goal

12 Using your head

14 Off-the-ball tricks

16 Tough tackling

18 Defending

20 Stylish dribbling

22 Superskills

24 The perfect goalkeeper

26 Goalies – diving and clearing

28 Solo practice

30 Fit for action

32 Index

Basic skills

When you play soccer, it is important that you feel comfortable with the ball at your feet. You can then develop decisive and confident ball control. The tips on these pages will help you become the boss of the ball.

Using your feet

This diagram shows the parts of the foot that you use when you play soccer.

Toe   Outside   Heel

Instep   Inside

Close control exercises

Stand still and put your foot on top of the ball. Roll the ball from front to back and from side to side under your foot.

Place the inside of your foot on the ground against the ball. Roll your foot over the top and down the other side.

Go the other way so that you are back where you started. Now repeat the exercise, using your other foot.

4

Using your skill

When you are playing in a game, you can use your close control exercises to turn with the ball.

Use the sole of your foot to roll the ball back behind you.

Turn quickly and move off in the opposite direction.

Running with the ball

In soccer nearly all the action takes place on the move. How you control the ball when you are running should vary according to your speed.

When you are running a long way with the ball, push it forward without breaking the rhythm of your stride. Don't push it too far ahead of you though, or you may lose control.

For sudden bursts of speed over short distances (and in crowded situations) use small, quick touches keeping the ball close to your feet. If anybody tries to tackle, you should tap the ball out of their reach.

When you have the ball, keep your head up so that you can see both the ball and the activity around you. In a game, you need to see the positioning of the other players.

5

Killing the ball

When soccer players talk about "killing the ball", they really mean stopping it, so that it is under their complete control. You can stop the ball with any part of your body except your arms and hands. Relax and bring back the part first touching the ball. This is called cushioning. If you are tense the ball will just bounce away.

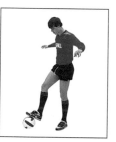

Sole of the foot

Point your foot up with the sole at an angle to the ground. Stop the ball, slightly in front of your body, so that you are in a position to pass it easily or start dribbling it.

Use this to control low passes that are coming straight at you.

Inside of the foot

Turn your foot so that the inside faces the ball. Then trap the ball between the ground and your foot. The inside of your foot should meet the middle area of the ball.

Use this technique to control low passes that are coming at speed.

Instep

Bend your knee and lift your foot so that it is under the approaching ball. On impact, quickly lower your leg, bringing the ball down on top of your foot.

Use this technique to stop a ball that is dropping from the air.

Thigh

Lift your thigh up and stretch out your arms to help you balance. As the ball comes down, quickly lower your leg to cushion the ball. It will drop to your feet.

Use this to kill a ball that is dropping from above waist height.

Chest

With your arms held out, push out your chest. As the ball touches you, quickly draw back your upper body. Your chest will stop the ball and it should drop to your feet.

Use this to stop a ball that is coming to you at chest height.

Head

Move your head forward to meet the ball. On impact, bring your head back, so that you put no power into the ball. The ball should drop to your feet.

This technique is useful if the ball is too high to be caught by your chest.

Stopping the ball with the chest. Be careful not to touch the ball with your arms.

Passing

The type of pass that you choose depends on how far you want to pass the ball, how fast you want to pass it and so on. Try to plan which type of pass to use as early as possible. Professional players often decide what to do with the ball before it reaches them. The information here should help you to decide which pass to use at the right time.

Inside foot pass

Turn your leg out and kick the ball with the inside of your foot. The ball will travel wherever the inside of your foot is facing.

This type of pass is the best if you want to ensure that the ball is delivered accurately to another player's feet.

Instep pass

Keep your toe down and your heel up. Kick the ball with your instep. Keep your head and knee over the ball, and keep your eyes on the ball as you kick it.

This pass is ideal for firm, low passes over a long distance.

Outside foot pass

Position your foot slightly to one side of the ball and push it away with the outside. Try to hit the lower area of the ball.

This pass is useful if you don't have time to get into position to make a pass with the inside of your foot.

Lofted pass

Place your standing foot close to the ball. Swing your leg back, lean back a little, and kick the lower part of the ball hard.

Use this pass to lift the ball over your opponents to reach a player from your team who is far away.

Volley pass

With the ball in the air, bend your kicking leg and keep your ankle firm. Now steer the ball in the direction you choose.

Use this pass when the ball is in the air and you don't want to stop the ball before you play it.

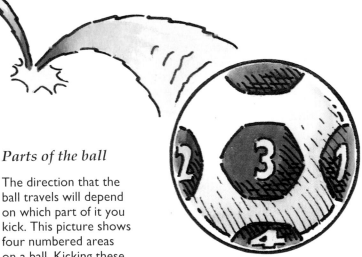

Parts of the ball

The direction that the ball travels will depend on which part of it you kick. This picture shows four numbered areas on a ball. Kicking these areas will affect the ball's movement as described on the right.

1. Swerves to the left.
2. Swerves to the right.
3. Straight ahead, keeping low.
4. Straight ahead, rising.

9

Shooting for goal

To win matches
you need to score
goals. Here are some tips to
ensure that you make the most
of your chances to score. When
you shoot, you can kick the ball
using any of the techniques that
you use for passing. It is more
important to kick the ball
accurately than to kick it hard.

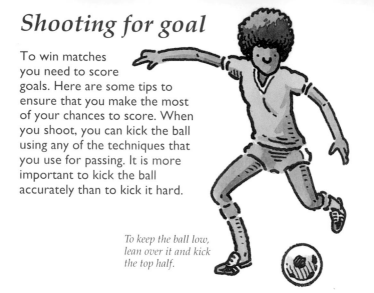

*To keep the ball low,
lean over it and kick
the top half.*

Placing your shots

Aim at the post farthest from the goalkeeper. Try to
hit shots low along the ground. With a high shot the
goalkeeper simply jumps to the ball. To save a ground
shot, however, the goalkeeper's whole body must
move from a standing position to the
ground. The ball may also be deflected
by bumps in the ground.

Maximum power

For maximum power
and accuracy, use
your instep when
you shoot the ball.

Instep

Following up

A shot may bounce away from the goalkeeper's grasp, so follow the ball after kicking it in case you get another chance to score.

Advanced shots

Volley

Shoot while the ball is in the air, without letting it fall to the ground. Use this when you don't have time to bring the ball under control.

Half volley

Shoot immediately after the ball bounces on the ground, just as it starts to rise. Use your instep and don't try to stop the ball before you shoot.

Swerving shot

Hit the ball hard close to its right or left hand side, using the inside or outside of your foot. The ball should swerve as it moves (see page 9).

Chip

Use this shot to lift the ball over a goalie who has strayed from his goal line. Stab the bottom of the ball with the front of your foot.

Using your head

If you are a confident header of the ball you can use your skill to score, clear the ball from your own goal or pass it to other players.

1. When heading, use your body as a lever. Keeping your eyes on the ball, pull your head and body back, then thrust them out to meet the ball.

2. Hit the ball with your forehead. Keep your body moving as you head the ball and keep your eyes open all the time.

3. As your head makes contact with the ball, clench your neck muscles so that your head stays firm and you can direct the ball away from you accurately.

Standing and jumping

When heading the ball from a standing position, you can improve your balance and ball control by keeping your feet slightly apart.

When jumping to head the ball, try to time it so that you head the ball at the highest point of your jump. This will give you more power and better control.

12

Heading for goal

Here, a header across the goal will give the goalkeeper little chance.

Always aim your headers as far from the goalkeeper as possible.

Headed passes

Flicking the ball across the goal often creates a good scoring opportunity.

A glancing header can divert the ball to one of your players.

Heading to score

When you head the ball at the goal always try to get your head over it. Aim it down firmly so that it bounces close to the goal line. This will make your header very difficult for the goalkeeper to reach.

The defender's header

Use lots of power and make sure that the ball goes up and over any attackers. Hit the bottom half of the ball to make it travel up.

13

Off-the-ball tricks

In soccer, you can be useful to your team even when you don't have the ball. For example, there are lots of things that you can do to help your team to keep the ball, build attacks and confuse opponents.

Positioning yourself

If you turn around to receive a pass from behind, you then have to turn back again to move upfield. To avoid this, position your body so that you receive the ball from the side. This will give you a better view of other players.

Player receiving ball.

Player receiving ball.

Restricted view of only one end of the field. Here, the receiver cannot see ahead to pass.

Wider view of both ends of the field. The receiver can spot defenders and who to pass to.

Moving into space

If one of your team has the ball, move into a space that could be useful to him. For instance, player 2 on the right should move into the space away from the two defenders so that he can continue Player 1's attack.

Player 2

Player 1

Overlap

If one of your team has the ball but is being closely marked, you can help out with the overlap trick. Run around behind the player with the ball and position yourself slightly to one side. If the defender tries to tackle, the player with the ball can pass it to you. If the defender attempts to follow you, he will not be able to challenge for the ball, leaving your player unchallenged.

The overlap trick can be very confusing for defenders.

Wall pass

Give the ball to one of your players and then quickly run around your opponent, ready for an instant return pass. You can use this tactic instead of trying to dribble around an opponent.

The ball is returned by your colleague, who is acting as a wall.

Crossover play

This tactic can outwit an opponent who is marking one of your players who has the ball. Run up close to them and run past. As you go past, your colleague has a chance to roll the ball back into your path.

Your opponent will be unable to see what is happening.

15

Tough tackling

To stop your opponents from building an attack on your team's goal, you need to be able to tackle effectively. Your aim is to make your opponent lose possession of the ball and, if possible, to gain possession yourself. The tips here should help you to improve this important skill.

Closing down an opponent

Closing down means denying a player the time and space needed to control the ball. Do this by quickly running forward to tackle the player.

Slow down as you get close to the ball, so that you will not be caught off balance if your opponent tries to sidestep you.

Jockeying

Having closed down, you can hold your opponent up before tackling, gaining time for your team to reorganize. This is called jockeying.

Jockeying can allow you to wait for a better chance to tackle.

Stand facing your opponent and block any runs. Be ready to tackle, as the pressure will force the player to make mistakes.

Block tackle

This is the most widely-used tackle. Try to stay on your feet after the tackle so that you can continue with the ball after winning it.

Close down your opponent. If you approach from one side, you restrict your opponent's movements in this direction.

Strike the ball just as your opponent tries to pass. Bend your knees and crouch over the ball so that your body weight is behind the tackle.

If the ball is stuck between your opponent's feet and your own, try flicking or rolling the ball over your opponent's foot.

Sliding tackle

This tackle is used to clear the ball from an opponent rather than to gain it for yourself. You could use it if you are unable to make a block tackle.

Approach from the side. Make your challenge before your opponent tries to pass. Take care not to commit a foul as you do this.

Tackle across the front of your opponent using your instep. Try either to push or to hook the ball as far away as possible.

You will usually be left on the ground after a sliding tackle. Try to get on your feet as quickly as possible, so that you can continue playing.

Defending

You must always guard against letting your opponents score goals. These tips will help you to defend successfully.

Marking

Defenders must be good at marking. There are two different styles: "man-to-man" marking and "zonal" marking.

Man-to-man marking

Zonal marking

Man-to-man marking

You are expected to stay close to one opponent throughout the game. You must stop the opponent from passing or shooting or being useful to his team.

Zonal marking

You guard a part of the field, marking any opponent who enters and trying to get the ball whenever it enters your zone.

Positioning

As a defender, you should never let the person you are marking get behind you. Try to position yourself behind your opponent, so that you can see where they move, enabling you to tackle them if they get the ball.

Defender behind attacker.

Here the defender can see his opponent and can challenge for the ball.

Attacker

Defender in front of attacker.

Here the ball can travel past the defender who must turn before challenging.

Defending free kicks

If there is a free kick near your goal, several players should form a defensive wall. The wall should protect one half of the goal, while the goalkeeper covers the other part.

The wall usually consists of strikers or midfield players, leaving defenders free for man-to-man marking. Players in the wall should not link arms as they need to break away as soon as the free kick is taken, in order to mark attackers.

Stand shoulder to shoulder.

The goalkeeper decides how many players are needed in the wall.

Shoulder charging

The only form of deliberate physical contact allowed during a game is called a shoulder charge.

Keep your elbow close to your side and nudge your opponent away from the ball using the top half of your arm against the top half of your opponent's arm. It is a foul to shoulder charge a player who is not within playing distance of the ball.

19

Stylish dribbling

Dribbling means running with the ball under close control, using quick, sharp taps to keep it moving. Skilful dribbling confuses opponents and makes it hard for them to tackle you.

Positioning the ball

Keep the ball slightly in front of you, so that you can see it and other players around you. Don't kick the ball too far ahead, though. A marker can intercept a ball that is not under close control.

Feinting

In soccer, feinting means confusing opponents by pretending to take the ball one way, but in fact going the other way.

Pretend to pass to someone. Your opponent may try to block the pass.

As your opponent moves, dribble around the player's standing leg.

Your opponent will be left off-balance, while you accelerate away.

20

Changing pace

When an opponent is about to challenge you, change pace suddenly. This may catch your opponent off-balance, allowing you to move away quickly without being tackled.

Changing direction

A change of direction can get you out of trouble if you become blocked by opponents. Don't worry if this means running in the wrong direction for a while. You can make up the ground when you have lost them.

Advanced feinting

This feint is fairly tricky to do because you will usually have to do it while you are on the move, sometimes at top speed.

Lean your body as though you are going to dart in one direction.

As your opponent moves to block you, shift your weight to your other side.

Push the ball to your other foot. Quickly swerve around your opponent.

Superskills

Use the skilful techniques shown here to beat your opponents and impress your team-mates. A word of warning though – they may take hours of practice before you can perform them properly.

Diving header

As the ball approaches at about waist height, launch yourself at it. Dive and hit the top half of the ball firmly with the middle of your forehead.

Use your arms to cushion your fall. Get up as soon as possible. These headers add an element of surprise to your game but at first they can be scary to do.

Walking on the ball

Diego Maradona used this trick while playing for Argentina in the 1986 World Cup Finals.

Drag the ball back toward you using the sole of your right foot. As the ball moves, jump and replace your right foot with your left foot.

Keep dragging the ball, this time with your left foot, while turning to face the other way. If you are left-footed, do the trick the other way around.

Cruyff trick

This trick is named after Johan Cruyff, who performed it while playing for Holland in the 1974 World Cup Finals. Try using it if you are being closely marked when on the attack. It is especially useful if you find that you are close to the edge of the field and you are facing the wrong way.

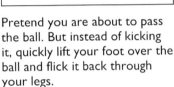

Pretend you are about to pass the ball. But instead of kicking it, quickly lift your foot over the ball and flick it back through your legs.

As soon as you have dragged the ball back, turn and move off in the direction you are now facing. Your opponent will be left standing.

Dummy turn

Do this trick to send opponents the wrong way. You'll have to do it quickly though, or they will not be fooled.

Pretend to kick with one foot, but take it over the ball. Put the foot that you pretended to kick with down on the other side of the ball.

Quickly turn and bring your other foot around. Then play the ball with this foot, either to pass the ball or to begin dribbling in a new direction.

The perfect goalkeeper

To be a good goalkeeper you need to be agile and to have sharp reflexes. Sometimes you will be the only person between your opponents and a goal, so you must be fearless too.

Palming the ball

Place your hand behind the flight of the ball. Use your palm or the tips of your fingers to help push it around the post or over the bar. Don't try to palm the ball if you are in the middle of your goal – you may not get it away from danger.

Collecting the ball

Use your body as a barrier. Turn your feet sideways to the ball and bend down on one knee.

Place your hands behind the ball. Your fingers should be spread and pointing down.

Catching body shots

When a shot is around chest height, place your body in line with the oncoming ball. Cushion the shot with your body. Cup your hands around the ball. Your arms and body should cradle the ball, so that it doesn't bounce away.

Catching high shots

When dealing with high balls, such as one coming from a cross, you should catch the ball as early as possible. Keep your eyes on the ball and jump to catch it at the highest point of your leap. Jump off one foot as you will be able to get higher this way. Place your hands behind the ball with your fingers spread out and thumbs nearly touching.

Turn your body so that it faces the flight of the ball.

When punching the ball, straighten your arms on impact to give extra power to the punch.

When catching a high ball, spread your fingers so that you can hold on to the ball.

Punching the ball

Using both hands, punch the bottom half of the ball as hard and as high as you can with your fists clenched tightly together. Aim to send the ball up over any attackers, away to the side of the field.

Goalies – diving and clearing

Always try to keep on your toes so that you are ready to spring into action if somebody shoots. As you dive, take an extra step to push off.

Push off with your left foot for a dive to the left, or right foot for a dive to the right. Try to get both of your hands behind the ball. Relax as you hit the ground and clutch the ball to your body so that it does not bounce away from you.

Avoid landing on your chest or stomach, or you may knock the wind out of yourself.

Bring your knees up and wrap your body around the ball as soon as you land.

Throwing the ball

Roll

Bend down slightly and roll the ball smoothly along the ground.

Shoulder throw

Bend your arm at the elbow and thrust the ball forward hard.

Overarm

With your arm straight, bring the ball back and swing it over in an arc.

Diving at an attacker's feet

If an attacker tries to race around you with the ball, dive sideways at it before a shot is made. Dive with your body level to the ground, so that it acts as a barrier.

To prevent injuring your head, do not dive forward head-first at the attacker's feet.

Smother the ball so no one else can get to it.

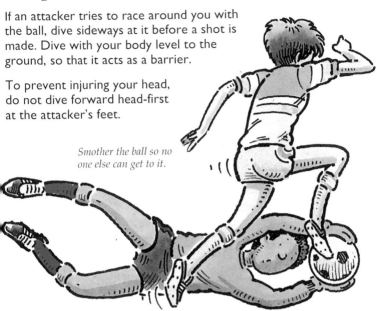

Kicking the ball

On the ground

Place your standing foot near the ball and kick it using your instep.

Volley

Drop the ball from waist height and kick using your instep before it bounces.

Half volley

Drop the ball to the ground and kick it as it hits the ground. This kick is tricky.

Solo practice

These practice exercises are perfect for sharpening your ball skills when you are on your own. They are ideal for helping you to become confident at shooting, heading, dribbling and passing. Try to beat the scores or times that are printed beneath each skill. You might like to challenge your friends, to see which of you can achieve the best score.

Two-foot tap

Mark two points about 12m (13yd) apart. Tapping the ball from foot to foot at least ten times, see how long it takes to get from one point to the other.

Good time: 15 seconds
Brilliant: 8 seconds

Foot-head

Mark two rectangles 1m (1yd) across on top of each other on a wall. The bottom square should be 50 – 100cm (20 – 40in) above the ground. Kick the ball at the wall, aiming at one of the targets. Then head the rebound at the other target. Try this ten times and make a note of your score.

Good score: 7 out of 10
Brilliant: 10 out of 10

One-foot wonder

Place eleven markers in a straight line about 2m (2yd) apart. Dribble between them using both sides of one foot. Turn and dribble back using your other foot.

Time yourself to see how quickly you can do this. Add five seconds every time you, or the ball, touches a marker.

Good time: 30 seconds
Brilliant: 25 seconds

Hotshot

Chalk out a rectangle on a wall, numbering different areas to shoot at from a distance of 11m (12yd). See how long it takes you to hit all of the areas in turn. As you improve, shoot from different angles and distances. To make it really tricky, return to area one if you miss.

Good time: 3 minutes
Brilliant: 2 minutes

Fit for action

To play your best soccer you need to be as fit as possible. Here are a few exercises that will help you to get into your best shape.

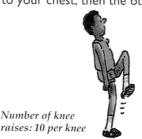

Warm-ups

Do these exercises before a game, or before you do more strenuous exercises.

Shoulder shrugs

Stand straight and raise both shoulders together, then push down.

Number of shrugs: 10

Knee raises

Stand straight with feet together. Slowly raise one knee to your chest, then the other.

Number of knee raises: 10 per knee

Windmills

Shake your hands by your sides, then slowly rotate your arms in large circles.

Number of rotations: 20

Toe touching

With feet apart, bend down and touch your left ankle with your right hand. Then touch your right ankle with your left hand.

Be sure to keep your legs straight.

Number of toe touches: 12

Strenuous exercises

These exercises will really get you breathing hard. After you've done them, you should do the warm-up exercises again, so that you give your body the opportunity to relax properly. If you don't, your muscles might become stiff.

Sprint and turn

Sprint for about 10m (11yd). Then turn around quickly so that your body is facing the other way and sprint about another 10m (11yd) in reverse. Take care that you don't crash into anything when you do this.

You will run a total of 60m (66yd).

Number of sprints: 3

Shuttle runs

Sprint 10m (11yd), then turn around and sprint back. Now sprint 20m (22yd) and return to where you started from. Continue to increase the distance by the same amount after each return.

The longest sprints you do will be 40m (44yd) each way.

Number of shuttles: 4

Push ups

Lie face down, with the palms of your hands beneath your shoulders. Keeping your body and legs straight, use your hands and arms to push your body up. Then lower your body so that you almost touch the floor.

Number of push-ups: 10

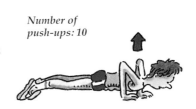

Index

Cruyff, Johan 23
cushioning the ball 6

defending 18, 19
  free kicks 19
defensive wall 19
dribbling 20, 21
  practice 28, 29

feet 4, 6
  using the sole, 5, 6
  stopping the ball 6
feinting 20, 21
fitness exercises 30-31
free kicks
  defending 19

goalkeeping 10, 11, 13,
  24-25, 26-27
  clearing 26-27
  collecting the ball 24
  diving 26-27
  kicking 27
  saving 24-25
  throwing 26

half volley 11, 27

heading
  defending 13
  jumping 12
  passing 12
  practice 28
  standing 12
  to score 13

Maradona, Diego 22
marking 18
  man to man 18
  positioning 18
  zonal 18

passing 8, 9
  practice 28
physical contact 19
positioning
  defensive 18
  of other players 5
  the ball 20
practice exercises 4,
  28-29
  foot-head 28
  hotshot 29
  one-foot wonder 29
  two-foot tap 29

running with the ball 5
  practice 28

shooting 11
  following up 11
  maximum power 10
  placing shots 10
  practice 28, 29
  swerve 11
  volley 9, 11, 27
shoulder charging 19
stopping the ball 6, 7
superskills
  Cruyff trick 23
  diving header 22
  dummy turn 23
  walking on the ball 22
swerving the ball 9

tackling 5
  block tackle 17
  closing down 16
  jockeying 12
  sliding tackle 17
  tough 16-17

This book is based on material previously published in *Improve Your Soccer Skills*.

First published in 1995 by Usborne Publishing Ltd, Usborne House, 83-85 Saffron Hill, London EC1N 8RT, England.

UE First published in America August, 1995.

Printed in Italy.